The Surprise Visitor

❧ by JULI KANGAS ❧

Dial Books for Young Readers  New York

DIAL BOOKS FOR YOUNG READERS

A division of Penguin Young Readers Group

Published by The Penguin Group

Penguin Group (USA) Inc., 375 Hudson Street, New York, NY 10014, U.S.A.

Penguin Group (Canada), 10 Alcorn Avenue, Toronto, Ontario, Canada M4V 3B2

(a division of Pearson Penguin Canada Inc.)

Penguin Books Ltd, 80 Strand, London WC2R 0RL, England

Penguin Ireland, 25 St. Stephen's Green, Dublin 2, Ireland (a division of Penguin Books Ltd.)

Penguin Books India Pvt Ltd, 11 Community Centre, Panchsheel Park, New Delhi - 110 017, India

Penguin Group (NZ), Cnr Airborne and Rosedale Roads, Albany, Auckland,

New Zealand (a division of Pearson New Zealand Ltd)

Penguin Books (South Africa) (Pty) Ltd, 24 Sturdee Avenue, Rosebank, Johannesburg 2196, South Africa

Penguin Books Ltd, Registered Offices: 80 Strand, London WC2R 0RL, England

Text set in Koch Antiqua * Manufactured in China on acid-free paper

1 3 5 7 9 10 8 6 4 2

Library of Congress Cataloging-in-Publication Data

Kangas, Juli.

The surprise visitor / by Juli Kangas.

p.   cm.

Summary: When a mysterious egg appears at Edgar the mouse's door,

he tries to find the right family for it.

ISBN 0-8037-2989-8

[1. Eggs—Fiction. 2. Mice—Fiction. 3. Animals—Fiction.] I. Title.

PZ7.K1277Ed 2005   [E]—dc22   2003021252

The artwork was prepared using ink, watercolor, and oil wash.

For Susan, Lauren, Bonnie, and George

Edgar Small sat down to write a letter to his brother. But he could not think of anything interesting to write.

"Dear George, it is rather windy today . . ."

He crumpled the paper. That's no good, he thought.

He didn't notice that a roundish object had been dropped by a gust of wind onto his shrubbery.

He didn't see it slide off and roll through the ivy, right down to his front door, where it stopped with a tap.

"Now, that's unusual," he said as he went to investigate. "A single knock at the door! Who could it be?"

When he opened the door, the object rolled right to his feet. "Well, hello, little, um, roundish thing. Where did you come from? You do look familiar. I think I've seen your ... roundishness before. I've got it! The Crustydomes! The Crustydome children all had your same sort of roundishness. How did you manage to wander so far from home?"

Edgar Small put on his jacket, bundled up the roundish thing,
and set off to see it safely home.

It wasn't far to the river's edge, where his old friend Mr. Crustydome
was busy at his easel.

"Mr. Crustydome!" he called. "You must have been so worried! But it's all right now—here is your little one, safe and sound."

Mr. Crustydome's wrinkled face became more wrinkled as he slowly spoke. "I beg your pardon, Mr. Small, but my children have long ago hatched and gone."

"Oh dear, then you're sure this roundish thing is not one of yours?"

"Quite sure," said Mr. Crustydome. "But don't worry, I will help you locate a mother for the little one. Someone will be willing to take the child in... especially if we give him a more attractive color."

He decided to use his *favorite* color, and when he had finished painting, they both agreed that it was a great improvement. As the paint dried, Mr. Crustydome tried to think of someone who knew a lot about raising children.

"Ah yes, Mrs. Twitch! There's a perfect mother for you, child!
Mr. Small, we're off to the meadow."

When they arrived and saw so many little Twitch children
playing in the meadow, Edgar Small felt sure that they had come
to the right place.

He introduced the roundish thing, and soon they were all playing together and getting along nicely. Edgar Small and Mr. Crustydome were so pleased.

When Mrs. Twitch appeared, they hurried over to speak to her.

"Good afternoon," said Mr. Crustydome. "Mr. Small and I were just taking a little walk. We've brought along with us a roundish friend who just happens to be in need of a mother."

Mrs. Twitch twitched.

"Just *look* at how well he gets on with your little ones!" he continued.

"He's remarkably quiet!" Edgar Small added. "He's no trouble at all."

"He does seem like a sweet little thing," said Mrs. Twitch, "but I really don't have room for any more! We should find someone who is actually *in need* of a child. And of course, something must be done about his face, to help him look a bit more appealing."

Mrs. Twitch got right to work on the roundish thing.

"Now, have a look at the little darling," she said. "Much better, don't you think?"

Edgar Small and Mr. Crustydome agreed that he looked much more cheerful.

Mrs. Twitch's face then lit up with an idea.

"My friends Mr. and Mrs. Chibble won't be able to resist this sweet face! And they will be so grateful for him, because they have no children at all."

She put the older children in charge of the household for a little while, so she could lead the way to the Chibbles' home in the forest.

When they reached the bottom of a very tall tree,
Edgar Small was surprised to see Mrs. Twitch stop and
point upwards. He doubted that she or Mr. Crustydome
was an experienced climber, but he was pleased that they
were willing to take on the challenge, for the sake of the
roundish thing.

When at last they reached the home of Mr. and Mrs. Chibble, they were very glad to be offered refreshments.

"My dear Mrs. Twitch," said Mrs. Chibble, "how marvelous that you and your friends were able to come and surprise us today! And how are the little ones? Wise of you not to bring them along. This house is obviously no place for a child."

"But," said Edgar Small, "we *have*, in fact, brought along this one very well-behaved and handsome child."

"Oh dear," said Mrs. Chibble.

"We're trying to find a family for him," said Mr. Crustydome.

"Egad!" said Mr. Chibble.

"Our neighbor, two branches up, seems very lonely lately," said Mrs. Chibble. "This roundish thing might be just what she needs for company. Let's bring him to her!"

"Just as soon as we fix him up a little," added Mr. Chibble. "We want him to make a good impression!"

Edgar Small allowed the two of them to carry the roundish thing into their kitchen, where they tried all sorts of things to dress him up.

Finally, they were satisfied. "The child just needed a tail, that's all!" said Mr. Chibble.

Everyone was quite relieved, and hurried up to introduce him to the neighbor, Mrs. Fleedle.

When they arrived, they found her in a very sad state,
circling around her nest and weeping.

"We've brought you something that may cheer you up,
Mrs. Fleedle," said Mrs. Chibble.

"Just look at this bushy-tailed nipper!" said Mr. Chibble.

"What a lovely smile he has!" said Mrs. Twitch.

"Yellow as a buttercup!" said Mr. Crustydome.

"No, no, you don't understand," sobbed Mrs. Fleedle. "What I really want is my own little Oliver back! He's been missing since this morning. Could you help me find him? He is so adorable—a bit bluish, somewhat speckly, rather roundish, and on the *inside*, he's—"

And at that moment she was interrupted by a crackling sound. A tiny head appeared, and a tiny voice said, "Mama?"

"It's Oliver!" sang out Mrs. Fleedle joyfully. "You see, he's even more adorable on the inside! How can I thank you all for bringing my precious child back to me?"

"There is no need, madam," said Edgar Small. "My friends and I are delighted to see the little one safely home with you." But Mrs. Fleedle insisted they stay for dinner.

After a lovely evening, Mrs. Fleedle helped her new friends get safely back down to the ground. Many thank-yous and good-byes were said before everyone cheerfully headed home.

As Edgar Small stepped through the doorway of his own warm and cozy house, he knew exactly what he wanted to do. He hurried to his desk and began to write: "Dear George, today I had a surprise visitor..."